Monst...
Don'...
Scuba Dive

There are more books about the Bailey School Kids!
Have you read these adventures?

Vampires Don't Wear Polka Dots
Leprechauns Don't Play Basketball
Santa Claus Doesn't Mop Floors
Werewolves Don't Go to Summer Camp
Ghosts Don't Eat Potato Chips
Frankenstein Doesn't Plant Petunias
Aliens Don't Wear Braces
Genies Don't Ride Bicycles
Pirates Don't Wear Pink Sunglasses
Witches Don't Do Backflips
Skeletons Don't Play Tubas
Cupid Doesn't Flip Hamburgers
Gremlins Don't Chew Bubble Gum

Monsters Don't Scuba Dive

by **Debbie Dadey**
and
Marcia Thornton Jones

illustrated by John Steven Gurney

A
LITTLE APPLE
PAPERBACK

SCHOLASTIC INC.
New York   Toronto   London   Auckland   Sydney

ISBN 0-590-22635-5

12 11 10 9 8 7 6 5 4 3 2 1   5 6 7 8 9/9 0/0

Printed in the U.S.A.   40

First Scholastic printing, May 1995

Book design by Laurie Williams

For Theresa Dadey, Betty Gibson, Michelle Dadey, and Melissa Thornton.

Four wonderful ladies who have monsters for sisters-in-laws.

Contents

Monsters Don't Scuba Dive

1

Vacation

"This is *not* how I want to spend my vacation!" Eddie complained and stuck his head out the bus window. His baseball cap almost blew off, so he pulled it tighter over his curly red hair.

Howie nodded without looking up from his book. "I wanted to stay home and finish reading *Creatures of the Deep.*"

"Reading!" Eddie snorted. "That's all you think about. What's so great about that book anyway?"

Howie held up the brand-new book he'd bought with his allowance. "It's all about monsters lurking in the water!" Howie exclaimed. "I bet you'd even like it."

"You have monsters lurking in your head if you think I'm going to read a

book during my vacation," Eddie told him.

"I think reading is a great way to spend the summer," Melody interrupted. "It's better than collecting mosquito bites at Camp Lone Wolf!"

Liza stuck her head out of the window in front of Eddie. "Nobody wants to go to this camp, but we might as well make the best of it." Their entire bus was loaded with kids from Bailey City heading for the nearby camp.

"Liza's right. We should have a better attitude. I bet camp will be lots of fun," Melody said. "We should be getting close now. Can you see the sign yet?"

"All I can see is blonde hair," Eddie complained to Liza. "Get this mop off me before I take out my scissors."

Liza pulled her head inside the bus. "Don't be such a grouch. My hair didn't hurt you."

"It hurts me just to look at her," Eddie

muttered to his best friend Howie.

Howie ignored Eddie and pointed out the window. "There's the sign, we're almost there."

"Thank goodness," Melody said. "Bouncing on this bus is giving me a stomachache."

Eddie bopped her on the head with his ball cap. "I *told* you not to drink that chocolate milk on the bus. Now, you're nothing but a big milkshake," he teased.

"Ha-ha!" Melody sneered. "If someone gave you a joke book you might even be funny."

Eddie started to say something back, but instead he looked out the window. A brand-new stone sign read *Welcome to Camp Lone Wolf: A Home for Every Plant and Creature.*

"Look, Eddie," Melody teased. "We finally found a place where you're welcome."

This time Eddie did say something back to Melody, but nobody on the bus heard what he said. All they heard was strange music. Strange loud music.

"What is that racket?" yelled Liza, holding her hands to her ears.

"It's bagpipe music!" Howie screamed back. Only the music had stopped and his scream echoed throughout the bus. Every kid on the bus turned to look at Howie.

Howie shrugged and turned red. "It's bagpipe music," he said again, this time quietly.

"No bird made that music," Eddie said, shaking his head.

"No." Melody giggled. "A bagpipe isn't a bird, it's a musical instrument from Scotland. Don't you remember anything from music class?"

"I knew that," Eddie said quickly. "But what's a bagpipe doing way out here in the middle of nowhere?"

Liza pointed out the window at a pale slender woman. She was dressed in a wet suit, face mask, and green flippers. Slung over her shoulder was a bagpipe. "There's where the music came from," Liza said as the bus came to a stop.

"Now I've seen everything," Eddie said, rolling his eyes. "A sea monster playing the bagpipes."

2

Too Cold to Swim

Mr. Jenkins greeted them at the bus door. Even though the kids had been to Camp Lone Wolf before, they couldn't get used to the hairy camp director. Mr. Jenkins had hair everywhere, like a wolf. Some of the kids even thought he might be a werewolf.

"Welcome to Camp Lone Wolf, you city slickers," Mr. Jenkins bellowed in a voice so loud it rattled the bus windows. "Before I give your cabin assignments, I'd like you to meet the camp's new swimming instructor."

"Swimming?" Eddie asked. "It's too cold to swim. I'd turn into an ice cube."

"No talking in the ranks," Mr. Jenkins bellowed, causing his dog tags to jingle. He turned to the lady beside him and smiled. "This is Nessie, Nessie McFarland. She's a very special guest here from Scotland and she's offered to teach you guppies how to snorkel and swim."

"Wow!" Howie gasped. "I've always wanted to snorkel." Several other kids in the group nodded in agreement.

"I've always wanted to stay home for my vacation," Eddie complained, but he got quiet when Mr. Jenkins glared at him.

Mr. Jenkins patted Nessie McFarland on the arm and all the kids waited for her to speak. She was silent for a moment while everyone watched her. Nessie was thin and tall, even taller than Mr. Jenkins. Her face was so white, it looked like she'd never seen the sun, and her neck looked like someone had stretched it. She was wearing a black wet suit and holding a set of bagpipes. Her hands shook on the bagpipes like she was nervous.

"W—welcome my ladies and gents," Nessie said in a soft voice that sounded

musical, like a song from a faraway land. "I look forward to teaching you about the beauties of the deep. 'Tis a joy I'm honored to share."

Mr. Jenkins smiled at Nessie and then scowled at the kids. "Listen up for your cabin assignments. I'll only give them once." Mr. Jenkins quickly called out the cabin assignments. Melody, Liza, and six other girls were in Cabin Gray Wolf. Eddie and Howie were together in Cabin Silver Wolf along with seven other boys.

"Stow your gear, then meet at the dock," Jenkins bellowed to the kids as they hoisted their bags and headed for the cabins to store their stuff.

"I can't wait to try out snorkeling," Howie told his friends.

"It sounds scary to me," Liza whimpered.

Eddie rolled his eyes. "The only thing scary are the icicles we'll have to break off our noses. I still say it's too cold for swimming."

Melody giggled and adjusted her backpack. "I bet Mr. Jenkins doesn't notice if it's cold or not. I think he's too much in love."

"Love?" Eddie said. "Why would you think that?"

"Didn't you see the way he looked at Nessie McFarland?" Melody asked.

Liza nodded. "It's so romantic. I bet she came all the way from Scotland just to be with Mr. Jenkins."

"Oh, brother." Eddie pretended to gag. "I think I'm going to be sick."

"Do it in the bathroom," Howie suggested. "Here are the cabins."

Melody jumped up and down, bouncing her black braids. "A bathroom," she shouted. "Just what I need. Look out!" Melody dropped her bag and ran into Cabin Gray Wolf.

Liza grinned and picked up Melody's

bag. "It looks like we're in for another interesting week at Camp Lone Wolf."

"Don't you mean boring?" Eddie asked.

"Oh, no," Howie shook his head. "Camp Lone Wolf is anything but boring."

3

Safe and Sound at Camp Lone Wolf

Nessie McFarland was already at the dock by the time the kids got there. She looked like a skinny seal perched at the end of the wooden pier with her bagpipes resting beside her. Her black wet suit glistened, and one of her long green flippers gently swished in the water.

"She looks like something that washed up from the ocean floor," Eddie giggled.

"Shhh," Liza warned. "Be nice. She looks a little nervous."

"Mr. Jenkins told us to meet you down here," Melody said in her most polite voice.

Miss McFarland cleared her throat and nodded. "Of course," she said in her sing-song accent. "I will be teaching you about swimming in these beautiful waters."

"The water doesn't look beautiful to me," Eddie interrupted. "It's cloudy green and it used to be blue."

Miss McFarland gazed across the lake for a full minute before she answered. "Perhaps from here it is hard to see the beauty. But there are riches to be found beneath the waters."

"Do you mean we'll find more treasure?" Liza squealed.

Nessie McFarland looked confused.

"When we came to Camp Lone Wolf on a nature retreat, we found out that a pirate hid treasure on the shores of the Red River," Melody explained.

Liza jumped up and down. "I bet some of the treasure drifted into this lake."

"There's no pirate's treasure beneath the waters of this loch," Nessie McFarland blurted.

"A lock?" Eddie interrupted.

"Lake," Howie said softly. "That's what

16

a lake is called in Scotland. It's spelled l-o-c-h."

"Why did you come all the way from Scotland to Camp Lone Wolf?" Melody asked.

Nessie's cheeks turned the color of a sunburn as she slipped into the water without making a single splash. She disappeared beneath the water for a moment, then surprised the kids by popping her head up on the other side of the dock. "I like the waters of Loch Erin," she told the kids. "It is so much calmer and safer than where I am from."

"If you're from Scotland, then you wouldn't know anything about the pirate's treasure," Eddie told her. "Someone would have to swim every inch of this lake to find any treasure. That's just what I'm going to do."

"I thought it was too cold," Melody reminded him.

"When it comes to treasure nothing is too cold," Eddie said. "Let's get started."

"Not so fast," rumbled a voice from behind the kids. It was Mr. Jenkins rubbing his beard. "No one's dipping a single paw into Lake Erin until you learn a thing or two."

Eddie groaned. "But this is our vacation. We shouldn't have to learn a doggone thing!"

Mr. Jenkins rubbed his beard and looked at Eddie. Melody gasped and Liza

closed her eyes, expecting Eddie to become a doggy treat for the wolflike Mr. Jenkins. But their hairy camp director smiled, showing his eyeteeth. They looked like fangs, and goose bumps popped up on Melody's arms.

"Go ahead then," Mr. Jenkins dared Eddie. "Jump in."

Eddie put his hands on his hips. "I think I will. I already know how to swim!" With that, Eddie walked to the end of the dock.

"You better test the water first," Mr. Jenkins warned.

"Why?" Eddie asked. "After all, Miss McFarland jumped right in." Eddie pointed to the lake where Miss McFarland had been. But now she was nowhere to be seen.

"Hey!" Liza called out. "Where did she go?"

"Nobody swims that quietly," Melody whispered.

"Not unless they're very used to the water," Howie said slowly.

"Exactly," barked Mr. Jenkins. "Which is why you need to learn a few things. Go ahead, Eddie. Stick that big toe of yours into the water."

Eddie shrugged and kerplunked his foot into Lake Erin. But it didn't stay in very long because Eddie hopped back, splashing water all over the dock. "Yikes! That water is as cold as the Abominable Snowman's nose! How can Miss McFarland stand it?"

Mr. Jenkins smiled again. "I'm glad you asked. Have a seat and I'll teach you a few things about this lake."

The sun was low in the sky by the time Mr. Jenkins finished showing the kids about the wet suits that would keep them warm in icy waters and how to breathe through the tube when they snorkeled, a kind of diving. "You will enjoy exploring below the surface of the waters," Mr. Jenkins told the kids. "There are so many fascinating things to see in nature. That's why I decided to make Camp Lone Wolf a sanctuary where animals and plants can live without fear."

"There aren't any interesting animals in these old woods," a fat boy named Huey complained.

Mr. Jenkins rubbed his beard. "When animals find out they can be safe and sound at Camp Lone Wolf, they will find their way here."

"What kind of animals?" Liza asked.

Mr. Jenkins spoke softly. "All kinds of animals."

"Like werewolves." Eddie giggled, but he grew quiet when Mr. Jenkins glared at him.

"There will be animals of the forest," Mr. Jenkins continued, "and creatures of the deep."

Howie gulped when he heard the name of his book. But he didn't get a chance to say anything, because just then something made a big splash right in the middle of Lake Erin.

4

Creature of the Deep

"What was that?" Liza shrieked.

Mr. Jenkins gazed out to the center of the lake where they had heard the huge splash. It was a long time before he turned back and smiled, showing his two eyeteeth. "There is nothing to fear. I'm sure it was just something fishing for its dinner. That reminds me, I want everyone in the dining hall in exactly fifteen minutes."

Mr. Jenkins glanced back at the lake, then marched toward the cabins. The rest of the kids followed.

"Let's go," Liza told her friends. "I'm starving."

Howie reached out and grabbed her arm. "Not so fast," he warned. "We need to talk. I have a very strange feeling."

"That's probably hunger pains," Eddie laughed. "Liza's right. It's time to eat."

"Eating can wait," Howie told his friends.

"Only if this is very important," Liza snapped.

Howie looked at each of his friends before answering. "The future of Camp Lone Wolf is in jeopardy."

"What are you talking about?" Melody asked. "Camp Lone Wolf looks better than ever."

Liza nodded. "You heard what Mr. Jenkins said. He's making this land a sanctuary for animals."

"But what if those animals are monsters?" Howie hissed.

"MONSTERS?" his three friends asked at once.

Melody shook her head so hard her braids slapped her on the nose. "There are no monsters at Camp Lone Wolf."

"Not unless you count Eddie," Liza giggled.

"Very funny, monster breath," Eddie snapped.

"This is not a joking matter," Howie warned his friends. "I should know because it's all in my new book, *Creatures of the Deep*."

"What's in that book?" Liza asked. "You're not making any sense."

Howie sat down on a nearby rock and waited for his three friends to sit on the ground. "It didn't make any sense to me, either. At least not at first. For many years, there have been reports about the existence of a monster. A creature of the deep!"

"Where is this monster supposed to live?" Eddie asked in a voice that let his friends know he didn't believe a single word of Howie's story.

"There were many sightings at a lake

in Scotland, but they don't call them lakes there. They call them lochs."

"That's what Miss McFarland called the lake!" Liza shrieked.

Howie nodded. "When scientists started studying those waters with powerful equipment, they found something huge moving along the bottom of Loch Ness. But lately, they haven't found a thing. Many people believe the monster moved away because there were too many people invading its home. They believe the scientists' loud noises scared it away. I don't think the monster is there anymore, either."

"They can't find it because it doesn't exist," Eddie told Howie.

"But there are pictures of the creature," Howie said. "The mysterious creature is very shy, so it often fled to the depths of Loch Ness where it lived, but a few people were able to see it."

"What did it look like?" Liza asked.

Howie took a deep breath. "It's black, skinny, and has a long thin neck with a little head."

Eddie laughed. "That sounds just like the new swimming coach!"

"Exactly!" Howie hissed. "I think the Loch Ness monster has fled Scotland and she's right here in the waters of Lake Erin. And her name is Nessie McFarland!"

5

Fishy

"Are you bonkers?" Eddie shook his head. "Nessie McFarland is a nervous lady, but she's no monster."

"Don't you think it's strange that her name is Nessie?" Howie asked.

"Just like Loch *Ness*!" Liza said, her face turning pale.

"It was pretty weird about her disappearing," Melody said slowly. "She never came back out of the water."

"Sure she did," Eddie said. "I bet she came out while we were talking to Mr. Jenkins. She's probably up there eating supper right now. Which, by the way, is where I'd like to be."

"I never saw her get out," Liza whispered.

"You never saw her, because she's the

one who made that big splash in the water," Howie said.

"I'm getting scared," Liza whimpered.

"Come on, Liza," Eddie grabbed Liza's arm. "Let's get out of here before Howie has us dancing with swamp monsters and mermaids."

Liza and Eddie walked up the path next to Lake Erin with Melody and Howie following. Suddenly, there was a big splash in the lake right beside them. Liza screamed and started running. She ran

the whole way to the dining hall with her three friends close behind.

"Why did you run?" Eddie gasped, when he'd caught up with her inside the dining hall.

Liza's face was red from running and she was panting. "I heard the monster in the water," she gasped.

Eddie rolled his eyes. "I told you, there is no monster. Howie's just making up stories. He should write a book instead of scaring you with his imagination."

Liza shuddered. "You may be right, but I'd feel safer away from the water. Far from Lake Erin. Like at home! And that's where I plan to go!"

"Mr. Jenkins won't take you," Melody told her.

Liza put her hands on her hips. "Then I'll call my mother. She'll come and get me." With that, Liza stomped off to the telephone.

"Oh, no!" Howie groaned. "Her mother

is the biggest blabbermouth in all of Bailey City. Now everyone will know about Nessie."

Eddie looked confused. "If there really is a monster, shouldn't you warn people about it?"

Howie looked at Eddie and Melody. Then he spoke seriously. "Mr. Jenkins is right. Camp Lone Wolf is the perfect place for every creature to live in peace."

"Even if that creature is a monster?" Melody asked.

Howie nodded. "As long as nobody gets hurt by the monster, it's only fair we make sure the monster is safe, too."

Just then, Liza walked up. "Did you call your mother?" Melody asked.

Liza looked like she was ready to cry. "She wouldn't believe a word I said."

Melody patted her on the back. "I'm sure there's nothing to worry about."

Liza didn't get a chance to answer because Mr. Jenkins bellowed for them to

get their supper trays. "Hey, stragglers, come eat before it gets cold."

Eddie smiled. "Let's eat. I'm so hungry I could eat an elephant."

"How about a whale?" Mr. Jenkins growled as he handed them their trays.

Liza looked at her tray and groaned. "It's fish."

Mr. Jenkins looked at Liza. "Fish is good for you. I hope you like it. We're having it all week."

"I think I just lost my appetite," Liza whimpered when she sat down at a table with her friends. Liza, Melody, and Howie picked at their supper, but Eddie gobbled his down quickly and went back for seconds.

After supper, the kids sat around a campfire. Miss McFarland showed them pictures of different fish and told all about them.

"I've never seen a fish like that." Melody pointed to a picture of a spiked fish.

Miss McFarland smiled. "Few people have been lucky enough to see this beautiful fish. There are so few left, even in the deepest waters. 'Tis true. The deep is full of strange creatures in danger of extinction."

"Creatures like sea monsters," Howie whispered.

Later as the kids walked to their cabins they heard a bagpipe playing in the distance. "That music makes me shiver," Liza said.

"I think that music has something to do with Miss McFarland changing into a monster," Howie said softly. None of the other kids said anything, but Liza walked a little faster.

It was starting to get dark and the sky was full of stars. In the pale light, the four kids saw Mr. Jenkins carrying a big pan out of the dining hall.

"That's the pan supper was in," Eddie said.

"What's he doing with it?" Melody asked.

"He's taking it down to Lake Erin," Howie said. "Let's follow him."

Quietly, they sneaked down the path after Mr. Jenkins. The kids watched as Mr. Jenkins dumped scraps from the pan into the lake.

"He's polluting the lake!" Liza said.

"Shhh, he'll hear you," Melody hissed.

"I don't think he's polluting," Howie said.

Liza shook her head. "It sure looks like it. Mr. Jenkins should know better."

"He knows just what he's doing," Howie said. "He's not polluting, he's feeding the monster." The kids watched as hundreds of bubbles filled the water where Mr. Jenkins had dumped the fish.

"Oh, my gosh," Liza squealed. "It *is* the monster!"

6

Monster Tracks

Bagpipe music woke the kids the next morning. Liza was still yawning when Melody dragged her into the dining hall.

"You look like you haven't slept in a week," Howie said when he saw Liza.

"I feel like it," Liza moaned. "Miss McFarland's bagpipe music kept me awake all night."

"I heard it, too," Howie said. "But she didn't play all night long."

"She probably took a nap," Melody suggested.

"Maybe," Howie said. "Or maybe she took a dive!"

"What are you saying, water brains?" Eddie snapped.

"Shhh," Howie warned, looking around to make sure no one was listening.

"Haven't you noticed that Nessie McFarland never plays when we're around?"

Liza shrugged. "Shy people don't like performing for others."

"You may be right," Howie said softly, "but I think she plays because she's homesick for Loch Ness. And when she gets homesick, she turns into a monster and returns to the water where she feels more at home!"

Eddie laughed so hard milk squirted out of his mouth. "Nessie McFarland is no monster. She's just a bashful bagpipe blower."

"But we saw the monster last night!" Liza shuddered.

Eddie shook his head and grabbed a plate of pancakes. "We never saw a monster. All we saw were bubbles. They could have been from lots of little bitty fish."

"I guess so," Melody said after sipping her milk. "I remember my mom and I threw bread to minnows once and they made bubbles like that."

"So there," Eddie said, licking his fingers. "This monster is just a bad dream. Let's concentrate on more fun things, like seeing if there's any treasure in the lake."

The kids finished their pancakes and hurried down to the lake. But Howie stopped short before they got to the water. "Look!" he shouted.

Eddie looked all around. "I don't see anything."

"Did you find some treasure already?" Melody asked.

Howie shook his head and pointed to the ground. "No, I found tracks. Monster tracks."

Liza's eyes grew wide. Melody and Eddie were quiet as they stared at the huge tracks in the sand. The tracks were as wide as a bicycle tire and shaped like a fan.

"A sea monster has been here," Liza said, backing away from the tracks.

Eddie bent down. "I don't believe it. There's got to be some other explanation."

Howie stuck his hand into one of the deep tracks. "There is only one explanation. And her name is Nessie."

"The Loch Ness monster is here!" Liza cried. "What are we going to do?"

7

Sea Monster at Large

"What would a sea monster be doing at Camp Lone Wolf?" Melody asked.

"You heard what Mr. Jenkins said," Howie told her. "Once creatures find out how safe it is here, they'll come on their own."

Liza twisted a strand of her blonde hair. "But I thought sea monsters lived in the ocean!"

"Liza's right," Eddie yelped. "Sea monsters don't live at kids' camps and they don't take strolls along the beach."

"The Loch Ness monster does," Howie told them. "And remember, Lake Erin is connected to the ocean by the Red River. I bet the monster escaped from Scotland when the scientists got too close. She came to Camp Lone Wolf to be safe."

43

"I want to go home," Liza whimpered.

Howie looked out at the lake and spoke quietly. "Once people find out there's a monster lurking in Lake Erin, they'll all want to see it. Camp Lone Wolf will be filled with curious people trying to see Nessie the sea monster."

Melody giggled and Eddie laughed so hard he had to sit down. "Listen to yourself," Eddie said. "You're talking like your brain is monster mush."

Melody added, "Miss McFarland is not a sea monster."

"How can you be so sure?" Liza squeaked.

Melody patted Liza on the back. "Sea monsters don't play the bagpipes."

"And they definitely don't scuba dive," Eddie added.

"I hope you're right," Liza gasped. "Because here she comes!"

The four friends looked up the trail. Sure enough, there was Miss McFarland.

She was dressed in her black scuba suit, and it was dripping wet. Mr. Jenkins walked beside her along with the other campers. Melody, Liza, Howie, and Eddie hid behind a clump of bushes until the group passed, then they joined the back of the line. They followed the trail onto the wooden dock. Liza and Howie hid behind the big kid named Huey, but Eddie pushed right up to the front.

"When do we get our feet wet?" Eddie asked Miss McFarland.

The new swim coach's hand trembled as she pushed a strand of wet hair behind her ear. "These waters will chill you at this time of year without the proper gear," Miss McFarland said. "Mr. Jenkins has purchased wet suits for you."

The kids raced into the nearby boathouse and pulled on the snappy black outfits. Once they were back onto the dock, they looked like a flock of skinny penguins. All the kids couldn't wait to try out the masks and snorkels. Everyone, except Howie and Liza. Liza hugged Melody's arm and whimpered, "I have a terrible feeling about this."

"Maybe it won't be so bad," Melody told Liza. "Remember, there might be some gold and silver scattered on the bottom. There's only one way to find out."

Melody hopped into the water along with the others. Eddie hollered and Huey did a belly flop. Miss McFarland covered her ears and turned as white as the clouds

in the sky. "Shhhh," she hissed. "Please stop the noise."

As the kids grew quiet, Miss McFarland took a shaky breath. "Everything sounds so much louder underwater," she explained.

"Did you hear that?" Liza whispered to Howie.

"I heard it," Howie told her. "And it doesn't surprise me one bit. After all, the Loch Ness monster is scared of loud noises."

"We better warn Mr. Jenkins," Liza said. "Before that sea monster nibbles us for lunch."

Howie nodded toward the water. "I think it's already too late!"

8

Jaws

All the kids, except for Howie and Liza, were gathered around Miss McFarland. She helped them practice breathing using their masks and snorkels. Soon kids were swimming all along the shore trying out the new equipment.

Eddie swam back and forth searching for treasure. He didn't notice how far out into the lake he'd gone until he got tired. Then he flapped his arms to stay afloat.

"Look," Liza screamed and pointed to the middle of the lake. "Eddie's drowning!"

Without even taking a breath, Miss McFarland ducked her long neck into the water. Her back arched as she dove deep and disappeared into the murky water of Lake Erin.

"Oh, my gosh," Melody cried. "I hope he's all right."

Liza clapped her hands. "He is! Miss McFarland's got him."

"I've never seen anyone swim that fast," Howie said softly. "And did you see the way she dove?"

"Don't start with that monster stuff now," Melody snapped. "Let's just be grateful Eddie's okay."

"Here they come," Liza said. All the kids helped pull Eddie onto the shore. Miss McFarland was right behind him.

Eddie pulled off his mask and snorkel

as everyone gathered around. "What are you guys staring at?" he asked.

"We thought you were going to drown," Liza explained.

Eddie shook his head and water splattered in all directions. "Don't be silly, I'm fine."

Miss McFarland pushed her mask up on top of her head and patted Eddie's shoulder. "Stay closer to shore for the rest of the week, just to be on the safe side."

Eddie nodded as Miss McFarland dove back into the water. He waited until she was on the other side of the dock, then he looked at Howie. "I don't know how to tell you this," Eddie said, "but maybe you were right."

"About what?" Howie asked.

"About the Loch Ness monster, you octopus brain," Eddie said.

"Oh, no, not again," Melody said.

"If you'd seen what I just saw," Eddie

said, "you'd believe in sea monsters, too."

"What did you see?" Liza asked.

"I saw something under the water. It was big, black, and shaped like a dinosaur," Eddie told his friends.

"Oh, no!" Liza squealed. "Wait until my mother hears about this!"

Eddie held up his hand. "Don't call your mom yet, because I have a plan!" he said.

"What?" Melody, Liza, and Howie asked together.

"We're going to catch us a sea monster," Eddie said with a smile.

9

Fishing for a Monster

Heavy dark clouds hung over Camp Lone Wolf the next morning, so Mr. Jenkins decided to go hiking instead of swimming in the chilly waters. While the rest of the kids headed into the forest, Eddie, Liza, Howie, and Melody sneaked down to the boat dock. Eddie jumped into a boat and threw on a life jacket. "Come on," he called to his friends. "Let's go fishing for a sea monster."

"How can you say that about Miss McFarland?" Melody asked. "After all, she did save you from drowning."

"In the first place, I wasn't drowning," Eddie snapped. "And in the second place she *is* a monster, isn't she? That means she's dangerous. Besides, we'll be famous if we catch the Loch Ness monster in action."

"Even if she is a monster, I think we should leave her alone," Liza said. "Everyone deserves to live in peace."

Howie and Melody nodded in agreement. Eddie jumped up and screamed. "Haven't you people ever seen the movie *Jaws*? Are you going to wait around until it's too late? I'm going to do something and I'm going to do it now."

Melody, Liza, and Howie were silent for a moment. They'd all seen the movie Eddie was talking about where a huge monsterlike shark attacks innocent swimmers. Howie shrugged his shoulders and spoke slowly. "I guess it wouldn't hurt to just take a look," he said.

"Now you're talking." Eddie smiled. The four kids settled into the rowboat with their life jackets and began rowing toward the middle of the lake where they'd heard the huge splash yesterday.

"I think this is the right spot," Melody told them after they'd rowed to the middle. The kids sat silently in the boat looking at the green water.

"Do you see anything?" Liza asked nervously after they'd waited a while.

"Nothing," Eddie said. "Maybe we need to use bait."

"What kind of bait do you use to catch a sea monster?" Melody asked.

"Fish!" Liza interrupted.

"Exactly," Howie said, reaching deep into his jeans' pocket and pulling out a crumpled bag. He dumped the contents into the boat, spilling little fish-shaped crackers everywhere.

"Those aren't fish," Eddie snapped.

Howie shrugged. "It's all I have. Maybe the monster will think they're real." Howie plopped a few of the crackers into the water.

"It looks like we've already caught one monster with our bait," Liza giggled and pointed. Eddie was popping a handful of crackers into his mouth.

"This whole thing is a waste of time," Melody muttered. "And to top it off, Mr. Jenkins will have our heads for not being on the hike."

Howie nodded and picked up his oar. "I guess you're right. We'd better get back. The wind is really starting to blow hard. It's going to rain."

"Wait!" Eddie shouted. He pointed to a dark shadow in the water. It moved right toward their boat.

"It's going under us!" Liza screamed and stood up in the boat.

"Sit down!" Melody shouted, but it was too late. The boat tipped over and the four kids tumbled into the storm-tossed water.

10

The Ride of Their Lives

When Liza's head popped above the water, she saw the overturned boat on the surface of Lake Erin. Melody, Howie, and Eddie had already grabbed onto it, but Liza was too far away. She bobbed on top of the water, floating further away from her friends.

"Swim over to us!" Melody yelled.

"I can't swim," Liza cried.

"You have to try," Howie called to Liza.

Liza tried. She kicked and slapped the water, but she didn't get very far. "Help me," she sputtered. "I can't get over to you."

"You won't drown," Melody screamed. "You're wearing a life jacket. But you have to kick your way over to us!"

"I'd better save her," Eddie said. But before he had a chance, Liza surged through the water, straight toward her three friends. In no time, she was close enough for Melody to reach out and grab her life jacket, pulling her to the boat. Liza hugged the boat so hard her fingers turned white.

"I thought you couldn't swim," Melody said.

Liza's eyes were as big as seashells. "I can't," she whispered.

"Then how did you get over here?" Eddie snapped.

"It was almost like something pushed me," Liza said. "Something big."

Melody splashed water toward Liza. "Don't be silly, it was probably just the current."

Howie shook his head. "It was Nessie, the sea monster."

"I want out of this lake!" Liza screeched.

"We all want out," Howie said, "A lake is a dangerous place to be during a storm!"

"It's dangerous when there's a monster in it," Liza whimpered.

"Maybe someone will hear us if we scream," Melody said.

"Exactly," Howie hissed. "Like the monster."

The four kids looked at the distant shore. "Look!" Eddie said. "There is someone on the dock."

"It looks like Miss McFarland!" Melody shouted.

"I'm getting tired of holding on," Liza said. "Maybe she'll help us!"

The four kids looked at the shore again. But no one was there. "Oh, no!" Liza whined. "Everyone must be going to lunch."

"That's exactly what we're going to be— lunch for the monster!" Eddie screamed.

Suddenly, the boat started moving like something had grabbed it from underneath. "It's the monster!" Howie yelled.

"Hang on!" Eddie screamed. "I think we're in for the ride of our lives!"

11

Peace?

The kids hung on as the boat moved steadily to shore. But once they were close enough to stand on the sandy bottom, the boat stopped.

The four friends scrambled to land just as a crew of men and women with TV cameras burst through the bushes. All of them held umbrellas over their heads as rain started to fall.

"Oh, no," Howie said. "Liza's mom must have told them about the monster."

Mr. Jenkins pushed through the crowd to Eddie, Melody, Liza, and Howie. "Nobody should be on the lake in weather like this!" Mr. Jenkins boomed. "You were supposed to be hiking!" The rain was falling harder and water dripped from Mr. Jenkins' tangled beard.

"It's not our fault," Eddie explained. "It was the monster's!"

"So there *is* a monster?" One of the television reporters pushed Mr. Jenkins aside to talk to Eddie. The reporter stuck a microphone in front of Eddie's face and a woman aimed a camera right at him. Eddie looked into the camera, then he looked at Howie. "See, I told you we'd be famous," Eddie said.

"Maybe," Howie whispered. "But what will happen if they find Nessie? They'll put her under a microscope. She'll never have any peace."

"She saved our lives," Liza added. "Everyone deserves a peaceful place to live."

Mr. Jenkins stepped up beside Eddie and glared at the reporters. "I don't appreciate your invading this camp and bothering these campers. I'm sure they don't have anything to tell you about monsters."

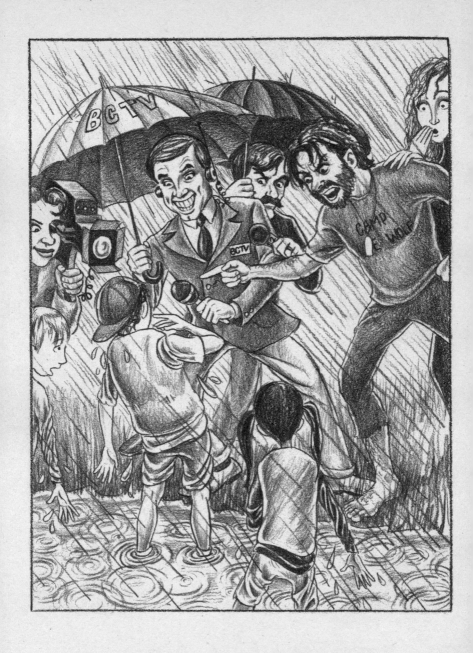

"Is that true, son?" the reporter asked. "Do you know anything about a monster in this lake?"

Eddie looked at Liza and Howie. He looked at Mr. Jenkins. Then he saw Miss McFarland come up beside Mr. Jenkins and put her hand on his shoulder. She was dressed in a wet suit. Water dripped from her hair and suit. She smiled at Eddie.

Eddie smiled back at Miss McFarland. Then he took a deep breath and spoke with the microphone right at his lips. "You reporters must be crazy. I thought us kids were the only ones who made stuff up."

Liza stomped up beside Eddie and pointed to the paper cups and cans the TV people had dropped on the ground. "I think the only monsters around here are the ones throwing their trash everywhere!"

The reporter's face turned red and he

took the microphone away. "Stop the camera. Let's get out of here."

Howie giggled as the reporters and camera people walked away. "I guess you guys told them."

"I knew there wasn't a monster in the lake," Melody told them.

"Of course not," Miss McFarland spoke softly. "But there's a great big hero right here on land." She leaned over and kissed Eddie's cheek.

Eddie shuffled his feet and shrugged. "I'd better go get some dry clothes." Melody, Liza, and Howie walked with Eddie toward the cabins.

"What happens if a monster kisses you?" Eddie asked.

Melody giggled and ran. "We'll find that out in about ten years if you ever get a girlfriend!"

Howie and Liza laughed. But Eddie didn't, he just chased Melody all the way to the cabins.

Debbie Dadey and Marcia Thornton Jones have fun writing stories together. When they both worked at an elementary school in Lexington, Kentucky, Debbie was the school librarian and Marcia was a teacher. During their lunch break in the school cafeteria, they came up with the idea of the Bailey School kids.

Recently Debbie and her family moved to Plano, Texas. Marcia and her husband still live in Kentucky where she continues to teach. How do these authors still write together? They talk on the phone and use computers and fax machines!